A Special Gift For

....

From

....

Just the Way You Are

ORIGINALLY PUBLISHED AS
The Children of the King

ILLUSTRATIONS
BY SERGIO MARTINEZ

MAX LUCADO

CROSSWAY BOOKS · WHEATON, ILLINOIS
A DIVISION OF GOOD NEWS PUBLISHERS

PUBLISHER'S ACKNOWLEDGMENT

The publisher wishes to acknowledge that the text for *Just the Way You Are* appeared originally in *Tell Me the Story* in 1992 and was released again as a separate book titled *The Children of the King* in 1994. *Tell Me the Story* was written by Max Lucado and illustrated by Ron DiCianni. More stories in the "Tell Me" series–*Tell Me the Secrets*, *Tell Me the Promises*, *Tell Me the Truth*, and *Tell Me Why*–published by Crossway Books, are available at your local bookstore. Special thanks to Ron DiCianni for the idea and vision behind the creation of the series.

Just the Way You Are

Text copyright © 1992, 1994 by Max Lucado

Illustrations copyright © 1999 by Sergio Martinez

Published by Crossway Books, a division of Good News Publishers, 1300 Crescent Street, Wheaton, Illinois 60187

Illustrations by Sergio Martinez

Design by David Uttley Design

First printing 1999

Printed in the United States of America

ISBN 1-58134-114-8

LIBRARY OF CONGRESS CATALOGING-IN-PUBLICATION DATA

Lucado, Max.
Just the way you are / text by Max Lucado.; illustrations by Sergio Martinez.
p.   cm.
Summary: A king adopts a family of orphans who try to impress him with gifts and their talents, but it is the one willing to spend time with him who wins his approval.
ISBN 1-58134-114-8 (alk. paper)
[1. Kings, queens, rulers, etc. Fiction. 2. Orphans Fiction. 3. Adoption Fiction.] I Martinez, Sergio, 1937-ill.

1I. Title.   PZ7.L9684JW   1999
[Fic]--dc21   99-16876
                                    CIP
                                    AC

08   07   06   05   04   03
————————————————————————
15 14 13 12 11 10 9 8 7 6 5

To Justin, Kindel, and Taylor

A long time ago in a land much like your own, there was a village. And in the village lived five orphans. A lonely family of fatherless children, they had banded together against the cold.   One day the king learned of their misfortune and decided to adopt them. He announced that he would be their father and would come for them soon.   When the children learned that they had a new father, and their father was the king, and that the king was coming to visit, they went wild with excitement.

When the people of the village learned that the children had a father, and their father was the king, and that the king was coming to the village, they were excited as well. They went out to see the children and told them what to do.

 "You need to impress the king," they explained. "Only those with great gifts to give will be allowed to live in the castle."  The people didn't know the king. They just thought that all kings want to be impressed.  So the children began preparing gifts to offer the king. They worked long and hard to be sure the king would approve.

One of the children who knew how to carve decided to give the king a wonderful work of wooden art. He set his knife against the soft bark of the elm and whittled. The small blocks of wood came alive with the eyes of a sparrow or the nose of a horse. ∽ His sister decided to present the king with a painting that captured the beauty of the heavens—a painting worthy to hang in his castle. ∽ Another sister chose music as her way to impress the king. For long hours she practiced with her voice and mandolin. Village people would stop at her window and listen as her music took wings and soared. ∽ Yet another child set out to turn the king's head with his wisdom. Late hours would find his candle lit and his books open. Geography. Math. Chemistry. The breadth of his study was matched only by the depth of his desire. Surely a king would appreciate all his knowledge.

But there was one sister who had nothing to offer. Her hand was clumsy with the knife, her fingers stiff with the brush. When the little girl opened her mouth to sing, the sound was hoarse. She wasn't much of a reader. She believed she had no talent. And so she believed she had no gift. ❧ All she had to offer was her heart, for her heart was good. She spent her time at the city gates, watching the people come and go. She would earn pennies to buy food for her brothers and sisters by grooming people's horses or feeding their animals. She was a simple stable girl. But she had a good heart. ❧ She knew the beggars by name. She took time to pet each dog. She welcomed home the travelers and greeted the strangers. ❧ "How was your journey?" she would ask. ❧ "Tell me what you learned on your visit." ❧ "How is your husband?" ❧ "Do you enjoy your new work?" ❧ She was full of questions for people because her heart was big and she cared about people. They were all the same to her—the beggars and the rich. She cared for all of them just the way they were.

But since the little girl thought she had no talent and no gift, she was afraid that the king would be disappointed. She remembered the villagers' advice and set her mind about the task of making a gift for the king. She took a small knife and went to her brother, the carver. ✍ "Could you teach me to carve?" she asked. ✍ "Sorry," the young craftsman responded without looking up. "I've much work to do. I haven't time for you. The king is coming, you know." ✍ The girl put away her knife and picked up a brush.

She went to her sister, the artist. She found her on a hill painting a sunset on a canvas. "You paint so beautifully," said the girl who had no gift but a big heart. "I know," the painter answered. "Could you share your gift with me?" "Not now," the sister responded with eyes on her palette. "The king is coming, you know." The girl with no gift then remembered her other sister, the one with the song. "She will help me," she said.

When she arrived at her sister's house, she found a crowd of people waiting to listen to her sister sing. ✑ "Sister," she called. "Sister, I've come to listen and learn." But her sister couldn't hear. The noise of the applause was too loud. ✑ With a heavy heart, the girl turned and walked away. ✑ Then she remembered her other brother. She took a book with small words and big letters and went to see him.

"I have nothing to offer the king," she said. "Could you teach me to read so I might show him my wisdom?"  The young sage-to-be didn't speak. He was lost in thought. The child with no gift spoke again. "Could you help me? I have no talent—" "Go away," said the scholar, scarcely moving his eyes from the text. "Can't you see I'm preparing myself for the coming of the king?" And so the girl went away sadly. She had nothing to give. She returned to her place at the city gates and took up her task of caring for people's animals.

After some days a man in merchant's clothes came to the small town.

"Can you feed my donkey?" he asked the girl. The orphan jumped to her feet and looked into the brown face of the one who had traveled far. His skin was leathery from the sun, and his eyes were deep. His kind smile warmed the girl's heart. "That I can," she answered eagerly, leading the animal to the trough. "Trust him to me. When you return, he will be groomed and fed."

"Tell me," she asked as the donkey drank, "have you come to stay?"

"For only a while. I'm looking for someone." "Are you weary from your journey?" "That I am." "Would you like to sit and rest?" The girl motioned to a bench near the wall. The tall man sat on the bench, leaned against the wall, closed his eyes, and slept.

After a few minutes he awoke and found the girl sitting at his feet, watching his face. She was embarrassed that he had caught her staring. She turned away. ✑ "Have you been sitting there long?" ✑ "Yes." ✑ "What do you seek?" ✑ "Nothing. You seem to be a kind man with a peaceful heart. It's good to be near you." ✑ The man smiled and stroked his beard. "You are a wise girl," he said. "When I return, we will visit more."

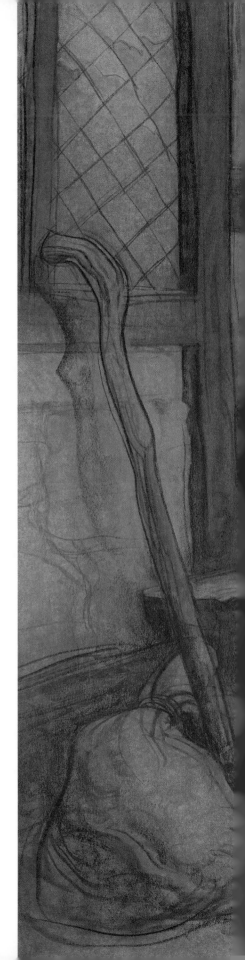

The man did return—quite soon. "Did you find the ones you were seeking?" the girl asked. "I found them, but they were too busy for me." "What do you mean?" "The first one I came to see was a woodsmith rushing to complete a project. He told me to return tomorrow. Another was an artist. I saw her sitting on a hillside, but the people below said she did not want to be disturbed. The other was a musician. I sat with the others and listened to her music. When I asked to talk with her, she said she had no time. The other I sought had left. He has moved to the city to go to school."

The girl's eyes widened as she realized who the man was.  "But you don't look like a king," she gasped. "I try not to," he explained. "Being a king can be lonely. People act strangely around me. They ask for favors. They try to impress me. They bring me all their complaints." "But isn't that what a king is for?" asked the girl. "Certainly," responded the king, "but there are times when I just want to be with my people. There are times when I want to talk to my people—to hear about their day, to laugh a bit, to cry some. There are times when I just want to be their father."

"Is that why you adopted the children?" ⁀ "That's why. Adults think they have to impress me; children don't. They just want to talk to me. They know that I love them just the way they are." ⁀ "But my brothers and sisters were too busy?" ⁀ "They were. But I'll come back. Maybe they'll have more time another day." ⁀ The girl hesitated. "Sir, what about me? I have no gift, but I would like to be your child." ⁀ The king smiled. "My dear, you gave the best gift of all—you gave your heart . . . your kindness, your time, your love. Of course you'll be my child. I love you just the way you are."

⁀ And so it happened that the children with many talents but no time missed the visit of the king, while the girl whose only gift was the gift of her heart became the child of the king.